The
Right
Prescription

The Right Prescription

Copyright © 2013 by Dr. Janine Scott, MD
ISBN: 978-0-9884899-3-6
Library of Congress Control Number: 2013932023
First Edition
Printed in the United States of America

2 4 6 8 10 9 7 5 3 1

Cover design & layout by Bryan Reed of liquid₂ Design – www.liquid2.com
Photography by Dalton J. Carter, Carter Multimedia Consulting, Incorporated
Editing by Duane A. Brown
Cranberry Quill Publishing, Inc.
111 Lamon Street, Suite 201, Fayetteville, NC 28301
www.CranberryQuill.com

About the Author

Dr. Janine Scott is a Family Physician who works at the Robinson Health Clinic on Fort Bragg, North Carolina providing medical care to the soldiers and family members of the 82nd Airborne Division. She is a member of the American Academy of Family Physicians and the North Carolina Academy of Family Physicians. She owns a nonprofit business called "All Things Encouraging" and hosts a website by the same name www.allthingsencouraging.com. There you will find helpful sections such as *Nuggets of Inspiration*, *Divine Inspirations in Prayer*, *Destiny Dreams*, and a daily *All Things Encouraging* devotional blog. She also hosts PPD - Prayer, Praise and Dreams - a quarterly get2gether women's fellowship meeting, and is a participant and host of the *Colors of His Love* Women's Conference.

Dr. Scott's publishing credits include: A review article in the American Family Physician, called "Raloxifene; A Selective Estrogen Receptor Modulator", September, 1999; a column in the Christian newspaper, *By Faith News*, titled *All Things Encouraging*; a letter published in "We Support You: Letters of Encouragement for Our Troops Serving in Iraq and Afghanistan." She recently became a writer and medical columnist for the *Beautifully Inspired Women's Magazine*, for women over 40 (www.biwmagazine.com). She is also the author of two devotional books entitled, *Reflections* and *Inspirations* published by Xulon Press.

Dr. Scott has been honored to receive the Health Outreach Award at the Lamplighter's Award ceremony, sponsored by the Raleigh, North Carolina inspirational radio station, 103.9FM, The Light. This award recognizes individuals, groups, churches and organizations that perform exemplary community service.

Her proudest accomplishment is being a mother of her two daughters, Kendall and Katrina Lowe.

Dedication

To my parents, my daughters, and my love…four earthly angels and one heavenly one.
All are the wind beneath my wings. I love you!
JS

Disclaimer:

The views expressed in this book are those of the author, and are for educational purposes only. They are not intended to circumvent the need for formal evaluation and treatment by a healthcare provider.

The **Right** Prescription

Even Christians Get Depressed

Even Christians get depressed. How do I know? I am a Christian, and I have been depressed. This sentence seems like an oxymoron, doesn't it? I have heard so many things said…"a Christians should never be depressed,""the joy of the Lord should be your strength—why don't you have joy?", or "you just need to have more faith and trust God more, just shake it off, everything is going to be ok." You know what? Yes, everything is going to be okay, but everything is not ok all of the time, either for Christians or for those who are not. Hearing these phrases, mostly given by well-meaning people, didn't help my depression, but made it even worse. Now I started questioning my relationship with the Lord. Yes, I knew I was saved, but I thought that somehow I was weak, or less than. There was "something" I wasn't doing right. I felt like I was letting the Lord down by not being a good witness for Him. Who would want to be saved or to have a relationship with the Lord if it didn't seem to be impacting me enough to keep me from being depressed?

I think before we can proceed further with talking about depression and the factors that can contribute to it, we need to address the idea of Christianity and depression. Unfortunately, there is a stigma concerning any mental health issue, even in the secular world, but even more so in the church. It is just something that is not discussed or talked about, and if it is, it is seen as a sign of weakness or deficiency. These ideas make it worse for a Christian suffering from depression, because where they would normally go to receive help, support and strength, they may feel they cannot; to not appear weak or like a "lesser Christian." What should be a haven and place of healing is denied, causing the depressed person to continue to keep on their "blessed and highly favored" mask, all the while suffering on the inside. It is amazing how those with other physical ailments (like high blood pressure, diabetes, or cancer) can receive compassion from others, but those with emotional or mental ailments cannot. Is one part of the body, if affected, more important than the others? We must remember that we are triune beings. We are spirit, have a soul (comprised of our mind, will and emotions), and we live in a physical body. Any abnormality in any of these areas causes a problem to the whole. One aspect is not more important than the other. Like the Body of Christ is described as many members, but one body, interconnected and interdependent, working together for the common good (1 Corinthians 12), so it is with each part of an individual's body. The different parts of the body are meant to work together. This includes the heart, lungs, feet, etc., but also the brain. If any part of the body suffers, the whole body suffers. Each part is needed to function as a whole and complete person.

Depression is a mental ailment that affects the brain, just as diabetes is a physical ailment that affects the pancreas. One part of the body is not more important than another.

Also, just because one is a Christian does not mean that they are exempt from the normal struggles of life (sometimes they may be affected by even more than their "normal share," because they are different and don't go along with the mainstream many times). No, the Word says that rain falls on the just as well as the unjust. We are all affected by sad or difficult circumstances at times. Should a Christian be depressed? Well, should a Christian ever be sick or have any ailment? Technically, the answer would be no, if we lived in a perfect state, as Adam and Eve did while in the Garden of Eden. However, when sin entered the world, so did sickness and disease. This was not God's perfect or original plan, but it is the state in which we live today. We live in a fallen world. However, as Jesus came to save us from our sins by dying on the cross by the stripes that He took on our behalf, we were also healed from all kinds of sickness and disease as well. That is the hope of the Christian. Whatever ailment we have can be brought to the Lord. Nothing is impossible to Him. He is Jehovah Rapha, the God Who Healeth thee. No matter what we may face or what affects us, when brought to Him, we can be made whole.

The **Right** Prescription

It is my hope that this book not only educates those reading it about depression and the various factors that can contribute to it, but also, that it puts a face on depression, such that it no longer remains taboo. I hope that the stigma is removed and discussion is begun. I pray that those reading this that may be experiencing depression will see that they are not alone. Many have felt the same way, and, best of all, that there is help and hope. As those in the book have come through, so you will too.

If you feel depressed, you are not alone. There is help and hope for you.

So, with that, we go into my story…

Janine's Story
He has made all things beautiful in His time (Ecclesiastes 3:11).
All things work together for the good of them who love the Lord and are called according to His purpose (Romans 8:28).

I was raised in a very supportive and nurturing Christian home. There were my parents, my two brothers, and me. I am the middle child and the only girl. And, I was smart. Before the age of 9, my dream was to become an air traffic controller, as that is what I thought that my dad did. When I found out that he was not (he was actually an electronic radar technician), I decided that I didn't want to be that, so, because I did well in school and assumed all smart people became either doctors or lawyers, I decided I wanted to become a doctor, and the path has not changed since. My grades were excellent, and culminated in me getting full scholarships to both college and Medical School.

After Medical School, I was accepted into the Duke, Fayetteville Area Health Educational Center in Fayetteville, NC for my residency in Family Practice, and was on my way to help and heal the world. Looking back on my pre-NC time, I have such fond memories. It's like I had the Midas Touch. At that time, everything that I touched and did seemed to turn to gold. One significant life event during my early years was when I accepted Christ as my Savior at the age of 6. I was raised in the church, and was surrounded not only by loving physical family, but by spiritual family as well. I was truly blessed.

But then, life changed. On June 6, 1996, I moved 13 ½ hours away from all that was near and dear to me, to Fayetteville, NC. I felt like Abraham; I had been called to move away from my kinfolk, to a land that I didn't know anything about, or anybody in the area. Talk about a significant life change! First of all, I had never lived away from home; in college, I was only 45 minutes away from my family, and I commuted to Medical School, while still living in my parents' house. Now, I had to establish my own place of residence. I no longer had the safety/security of family and friends, but had to meet new people and learn new ways. And, probably most stressful of all, I was embarking into a new stage of life, no longer being a student, but now in the working world as a physician. I began a grueling 3 year internship and residency, which demanded long hours and personal sacrifice to complete. This was certainly a stressful time, looking back. This stress culminated in me become depressed for the first time in December, 1996. The proverbial "straw that broke the camel's back," came when I didn't do well on a training exam during my internship. This was the first major test for me as a doctor, and I bombed it. I felt like I didn't measure up. I had always done well, but now I didn't. I didn't know what else to do, and I started spiraling. Everything just became so dark. I remember wanting to stay in my apartment with the blinds drawn. I didn't want to go out and do anything, or face anyone anymore. I cried all of the time. I felt overwhelmed. I felt like a failure.

In the midst of this depression, enter in someone who I thought was my knight in shining armor, my now ex-husband. At the time, he was very supportive of me. He kept me going. He called me each morning to make sure that I got up and was on my way, called me throughout the day to make sure I was making it ok, and then

The Right Prescription

called me in the evening to make sure I arrived home safely and made it through the day. He was my savior. My family and friends were there too, but they were so far away, there was only so much that they could do. My new friends were as helpful as they could be as well, but my ex was my major support, as well as my faith in God, that somehow I would be victorious in all of this, as I was doing what I believed to be God's calling on my life, and, because of that, He would see me through. Even with these supports however, it wasn't enough, as I couldn't seem to shake those feelings of inadequacy and failure. What did eventually help was counseling, that helped me to process all of the life stressors that had built up and toppled me over the edge into the depressive abyss. I also started to take medication to get me back on an even playing field so that I could function and thrive as I completed residency, and that's what I did (of note is that although I bombed that first exam, I scored highly on the next and continued to go on and pass the subsequent ones as well...things had turned around).

Fast forward a few years, and things were going reasonably well. My boyfriend became my husband, as we were married in 1998. We subsequently had 2 beautiful little girls. Unfortunately, the marriage ended in divorce 7 years later, and I became a single mom with its joys, yes, but also with its many stresses, as I now had to take care of things on my own. I continued to have problems with my ex over the years as well, and experienced increased stress and demands on my job as a physician. Another devastating blow was when I unexpectedly lost my mom, as she died on the table during a routine surgical procedure. Each of these stressors, on their own, were manageable at the time, but, as I kept going, and "doing what I had to do," they began to overtake me and have an additive effect on me. Over time, I started feeling run down. I became very tired throughout the day, but then couldn't sleep at night. I became very anxious and afraid. I started isolating myself, as I didn't want to be a drain or a "downer" in anyone else's life. I stopped finding enjoyment in doing what I would normally like to do. I was depressed again; it had returned. I finally hit rock bottom when I felt that the burdens of the world were too much for me to bear. I wanted to be a better mother. I wanted the best for my daughters, but I began to feel that I wasn't it. I wanted to simply go to sleep and not wake up.

It was at this point that I realized that there was a major problem. I needed help, and needed it fast. I couldn't go on like this anymore. I ended up being hospitalized for major depression. I had come to the end of myself. But, I am SO GLAD that I may have been at the end of ME, but I was NOT at the end of GOD. During this dark time, I really saw the LOVE OF GOD through others, who prayed for me, visited me, contacted me, and encouraged me. I truly lived the Scripture that said that even when I made my bed in the midst of hell, God was still with me (Psalm 139:8). There was nowhere that I could go that He was not already there. He was ALWAYS there, loving me, keeping me, upholding me, and guiding me. He held my hand as I walked through the valley of the shadow of death. He truly became love to me.

And, it is with this love and support that I am making it. Not having to be perfect; not having to be superwoman; not having to do everything on my own and being in control of it all. No, I am learning to take life ONE DAY AT A TIME, to DAILY lean on and rely on Christ as my strength, and to DAILY count the MANY blessings that I have in my life. The Lord has truly delivered me out of a pit, and continues to establish my goings. During my time of illness, I found God to be closer to me than at any other time. Truly, He was close to the brokenhearted (Psalm 34:18). I found comfort in knowing that He bottled up every tear I cried. I was thankful knowing that He understood what I was going through and that He was touched by my infirmities. He, Himself, was at all points tempted as I, yet without sin (Hebrews 4:15). I began to recover and get better as the joy of the Lord became my strength (Nehemiah 8:10).

And now, I want to help others to do the same. What you think is the worst thing you have ever experience can actually become

The **Right** Prescription

your blessing if you turn around and help someone else. I don't want my suffering to be in vain. Now having passed through the dark tunnel of depression and reaching the other side, I know that I can use my experience to encourage others, and especially my patients. Most of all, I want to give them hope. As the Word says, I want to be able to comfort others with the same comfort that I have received from God, leading them back to a place of joy and peace (2 Corinthians 1:3-7). That is what this book is all about.

He lifted me out of the slimy pit, out of the mud and mire; He set my feet on a rock, and gave me a firm place to stand (Psalm 40:2)

Janine Scott, MD

Rest, Eat and Drink—A Scriptural Parallel

Elijah's Story

1 Kings 19:5-8: And as [Elijah] lay and slept under a juniper tree, behold, then an angel touched him, and said unto him," Arise and eat." And he looked, and behold, there was a cake baked on the coals, and a cruse of water at his head. And he did eat and drink, and laid him down again. And the angel of the Lord came again the second time, and touched him, and said, "Arise and eat; because the journey is too great for thee." And he arose, and did eat and drink, and went in the strength of that meat 40 days and 40 nights unto Horeb, the Mount of God.

2 Corinthians 12:9: And [the Lord] said unto me, "My grace is sufficient for thee; for my strength is made perfect in your weakness." Aren't you glad that we have a friend in God? Aren't you glad that He knows us and understands our weaknesses? Aren't you glad that He is not a hard taskmaster, who drives us to our limits with no care as to our welfare or our continued strength?

Well, I am. These are the words that the Lord gave me one day during my study time with Him. It had been a tough week. Not anything particularly demanding or bad, just busy. You know how life gets; always something more you have to do, always someplace more you have to go. But, you push yourself and you do it. Why? Because you have to; that's just life.

Sometimes in the pushing, you may push yourself too far. I know I have a tendency to do that. I like to do many different things. I like to be active. I like to make sure I put my all into what I do, and do it well. I don't think that these things, in themselves are bad, but over time, they can tire you out. Yes, God does love it when we are active and available for and to Him, but He has also given us wisdom to know when enough is enough…when we have to rest. As it says in Matthew, His yoke is easy and His burden is light. There are times when we need to enter into the rest of the Lord.

The **Right** Prescription

That's where we are today. Elijah is tired, but not just tired, he is depressed and suicidal. As it says in 1 Kings 19:4, Elijah asked that the Lord allow him to die. He asked Him to take away his life, because for him, what he was feeling was too much; it was enough. Here was this prophet of God who had just been in an intense confrontation with 400 prophets of Baal. It was a showdown… whose god was truly God? Well, Elijah's God (and ours) proved true, as He sent down fire from heaven, devouring not only the prepared sacrifice, but even the water that was placed on it (God really showed out—He more than made His point, in case there was any doubt!) Elijah was the "winner," and the other prophets the losers.

So why was Elijah now feeling this way? He was just literally on the mountaintop, and now he was in the valley. What made him go from such an intense high to such a deep low? It doesn't seem to make sense. Perhaps it was because he was "riding high." His adrenaline had been pumping; he had the strength to do what he needed to do (even so much as to be able to kill the 400 prophets in the Kishon brook by himself! 1 Kings 18:40). But after the confrontation, after such a grand display of strength, he simply got tired. He was drained. He was empty. So empty that he felt like he couldn't go on—Elijah wanted to die.

What I love is God's response to Elijah's depression. Did God condemn him for being weak and lazy? Did He chastise him for his current emotional state? Did he think him a failure for not being able to go on? No! Not only did He not treat him this way, He actually did the exact opposite. God sent an angel to feed him, to provide him drink, and let him rest. I guess Elijah was pretty tired, because he was allowed to do this not once, but twice. God understood that Elijah's journey was too much for him, but thank God he was not required to go it alone; he had a heavenly friend, a ministering angel, to go with him, who strengthened him along the way.

I just love serving a God like that. He doesn't consider being tired or weak a bad thing; no, He nourishes us, refreshes us, encourages us, and gives us His strength to continue on.

So, if you are tired (whether physically, mentally, or emotionally), even so tired as to feel depressed or suicidal, God's word for you today is rest, but not simply to rest…rest in Him. Allow Him to minister to you and take care of you until you are restored. Receive the help and support that He sends your way, whether through friends, loved ones, physicians, counselors, medication or whatever. Truly, anyway God blesses you, be satisfied. Let Him be your strength while you are in your weakness, and receive His grace that is so sufficient to get you through anything that you must face. Rest, eat, and drink. Exchange your weakness for God's strength, and be restored to continue on with your God.

Depression: What is it?

Depression is a physical illness in which there is a depletion of certain substances in the brain (catecholamines). It seems to be related to a chemical imbalance in the brain that makes it hard for the cells to communicate with each other. It is thought that if you get hammered with enough difficult life stressors, the biology of the brain actually changes.

Enough stressors in your life can literally wear you out.
Depression is a medical illness with at least 5 of the following symptoms daily for at least 2 weeks:

1. No interest in things you used to enjoy
2. Feeling sad or empty
3. Crying easily or crying for no reason
4. Feeling slow or restless and not being able to sit still
5. Feeling worthless or guilty
6. Weight gain or loss
7. Thoughts about death or suicide
8. Trouble thinking, remembering things, or focusing on what you're doing
9. Trouble making decisions
10. Problems sleeping, especially in the early morning, or wanting to sleep more than usual
11. Feeling tired
12. Feeling numb emotionally, perhaps even to the point of not being able to cry

You may also have headaches, other aches and pains, stomach problems, and problems with sex. An older person with depression may feel confused or have difficulty understanding simple requests. Many times, a person is not only depressed, but anxious as well, as anxiety can coexist in 70% of cases.

The **Right** Prescription

This is not etched in stone. If you have these symptoms for less than two weeks and feel you need help, get the help you need.

People considered high risk for depression include those who have a personal or family history of depression (it seems to run in families), had recent stressful events (death of a loved one, a divorce, or a job loss), lack social support, have a chronic illness or pain, have unexplained physical symptoms, or who have alcohol or substance abuse. Also, taking certain medicines (glucocorticoids and reserpine) can lead to depression.

It is usually diagnosed by you telling your doctor your symptoms. He or she may ask you some questions about your symptoms, health, and family history of health problems, and may give you a physical exam and do some tests.

It can be treated with medicines or counseling, or with both. Medicines, called antidepressants fix the chemical imbalance that causes depression. They work differently for different people, and also have different side effects. You may start feeling better as soon as one week after you start taking the medicine, but you probably won't feel the full effects for about 6-8 weeks. Side effects of the medicine may occur at first, but they tend to get better after a couple of weeks. How long you are treated depends on your depression. Your doctor may want you to take the medicine for six months or longer. You need to take the medicine long enough to reduce the chance that the depression will come back.

Depression can usually be treated through doctor visits. If you have other medical problems that could affect your treatment, or if you're at high risk of suicide, treatment in the hospital may be needed.

You may feel bad now, but there is help. You will feel better again.

Dos and Don'ts When You are Depressed

- Don't isolate yourself. Stay in touch with your loved ones and friends, your Minister or Rabbi, and your family doctor.

- Don't make major life decisions (i.e. separation or divorce). You may not be thinking clearly right now, so your decisions may not be the best ones for you. If you must make a big decision, ask someone you trust to help you.

- Don't blame yourself for your depression. You didn't cause it.

- Don't be discouraged about not feeling well right away. Be patient with yourself.

- Don't give up.

- Do get involved in activities that make you feel good.

- Do exercise every day to make yourself feel better (4-6 times a week for at least 30 minutes each time is a good goal, but even less activity can be helpful), and eat right (follow a healthy diet) to get more energy.

- Do get enough sleep.

- Do avoid drugs and alcohol.

- Do take your medicine and go to counseling as often as your doctor tells you to.

- Do set small goals for yourself, because you may have less energy.

The **Right** Prescription

- Don't believe all of your negative thinking, such as blaming yourself or expecting to fail. This thinking is part of depression, and these thoughts will stop as your depression goes away.

- Do encourage yourself.

- Do get as much information as you can about depression and its treatment.

- Decrease the space here

- Do call your doctor or the local suicide crisis center right away if you start thinking about suicide.

Don't Give Up!

Watch Your Thoughts
"As a man thinketh in his heart, so is he." Proverbs 23:7

Condemnation:
- A Christian should never be depressed.

- Being depressed is a sign of weakness.

- Being depressed is a sign of demonic oppression.

- Being depressed means that you don't have enough faith in God to take care of you.

- You are a bad witness, and failure, to God if you are depressed.

- God is disappointed with you or punishing you if you are depressed.

Compassion:

- This is a fallen world. No Christian should have any problem or disease, but we do because this world is not perfect.

- Many times depression is due to being too strong for too long. Many stressors happening over a period of time can cause a depletion in brain chemicals (neurotransmitters), which can cause fatigue and depressive symptoms.

- Elijah was a prophet used mightily by God, and yet became depressed and suicidal. God didn't condemn him or punish him, but he sent an angel to take care of him, nourished him, and provided help to him by giving him others to aid him in his work. As God did with Elijah, He will do with you as well.

- Depression is not about your faith level. It has been your faith that has kept you going even when you didn't feel well. It is your faith that has kept you moving each day, and your faith that keeps you believing that you will make it through this time; it will not last forever.

- The best witness is not one who has never had any problems; people can't relate to that. The best witness is one who has had problems, but with God's help, has made it through and overcome them. Depression is not failure. It is not the end. It is a temporary situation that will get better with time and the help and support that God provides you.

- God does not condemn you, He loves you. He loved you so much that He sent His Son to die for your sins to bring you back into relationship with Him. Your depression is not a surprise to Him. He is omniscient and knows everything. He loves you no matter what, problems and all. And His desire is that you not remain in a state of sorrow, but He will turn all your sorrows into joy.

Janine Scott, MD

Depression is Equal Opportunity
It's not just a "woman's disease"

Will's Story *(Name has been changed to protect confidentiality)*
"This wasn't supposed to Happen to me"

There are three facts of life that have permanently left a boot print on the left and right sides of my behind.

1. Bad things can happen to good people

2. A broken heart takes time to heal

3. Depression does not discriminate on the basis of race, color, gender, religion, economic status or your role or title within the church.

That third fact is the one which keeps me grounded and humbled as I seek to do God's will. My bout with depression left me shaking my head saying, "This wasn't supposed to happen to me!"

In November 2007, I heard the words that no completely in love and devoted family man wants to hear; "I want a divorce!" This simple statement led to questions, tears, and arguments, which led to more questions, tears and arguments, which eventually led to a complete melt down and shut down of all communication and conversation. Whew, that was a rough first day! After five consecutive days I couldn't eat, couldn't sleep, and couldn't function at work. I was losing my two wonderful daughters, my happy home, and the woman who owned my heart. The hard part of it all was that I was the guy everyone looked to for encouragement, motivation, and to bring cheer their way. I was the guy who always had a smile on his face even when things seemed to be bad all around me. Do you know how hard it is to encourage someone else when you can't even find encouragement for yourself? For about a month, I would have to sit in my car and cry before going to work just to avoid crying while at work. I lost over 30 pounds in a month, and it was clearly obvious to everyone that my weight loss was not the result of Jenny Craig or Weight Watchers. As bad as I felt, it would have been very plausible to assume that I had become a crack head. Those were some very dark days for me during November-December of 2007. The pain and loneliness I felt almost got the best of me…..But God…..

Just when I had reached my breaking point and I began to feel that there was nothing left to live for, God stepped in and rescued me. Understand this, when you get to your lowest point and you feel that you have dug yourself into a deep hole, do two things: 1) Stop digging! 2) Look up! As I found myself quiet and still, I heard a gentle whisper that assured me everything was going to be okay. I recall sitting in my car and accidentally turning on the radio (Yes I said accidentally). I went to turn up the heat, and my hand mistakenly hit the power button for the radio. I heard Marvin Sapp's hit song, "Never Would Have Made It." As I listened to that song, I felt that God was telling me to give Him my problems. He was telling me to lean on Him and not rely on my own strength. I obeyed and here I stand today.

From that moment on, I centered my thoughts, my actions, and my life to serving God. I began to pray more often and read the Bible more consistently. It was amazing how the more I began to give to God, the brighter and better each day got. The message to me was clear; "Cast your burdens onto Jesus because He cares for you." I learned that a little walk and a little talk with Jesus makes it alright. Some may say that my heart break and the separation of my family is minor compared to the things others have had to endure. And you are right. Everyone's life is different and there are some awful things that happen in the lives of others. As I lived it up in my very own pity party, God sent a couple to me whose seven-year old son was dying from cancer. Two weeks after meeting this couple, their son died. I could not even fathom the pain this couple felt. It made my light and momentary troubles pale in comparison. Here I was crying and depressed because my children would have to live in another zip code, and this family just lost their child forever. I kept a photo of that little boy on the dashboard of my car to serve as a constant reminder to me anytime I felt sad or depressed. The message for me was this: "You better pick your head up son because it could always be worse."

My God-given purpose in life is to bring healing to everyone who God allows to cross my path. I realize that God takes us through trials and tribulations so that we may be equipped to help others. God heals us so that we can heal others. I pray that my story brings you comfort and healing. I no longer say, "This wasn't supposed to happen to me." I now say, "I thank God this happened to me." I have an awesome relationship with my two daughters. The time we spend together is so precious that the quality of the time totally outweighs the quantity of our time. I now realize that God had an even greater love He wanted me to experience. And if I had remained stuck in my past hurts, I would not have had an opportunity to experience it. If you remember nothing else from my life's experiences, please embrace this:

- If you are still alive today, God has spared your life so you can do a great work for Him.

- If you have found yourself in a deep dark hole, stop digging and look up to God.

- If you think you are having some serious problems right now, I can assure you that there is someone having it much worse.

Be Blessed!

Janine Scott, MD

Postpartum Depression: Not just the Baby Blues

Postpartum depression is a serious form of depression that comes after giving birth. As many as four out of five women have mood changes in the first 10 days after giving birth, usually called "baby blues." If the symptoms are more severe and last for more than 10 days, it is called postpartum depression. Some women feel better within a few weeks, while others may feel depressed for several months. Women who have more serious symptoms or who have had depression before may take longer to feel better.

Symptoms may include sadness, anxiety and crying. Some women worry too much about their baby, or may be afraid of making mistakes in caring for their baby. They also may find it hard to concentrate or fall asleep. Some women lose interest in things they used to enjoy.

Some women have pictures or thoughts pop into their mind about hurting their baby. These thoughts can be very upsetting, and do not mean that these women really want to hurt their baby. This is a common symptom of postpartum depression and will go away with treatment. Some women may think that life is not worth living, or that their baby or family would be better off without them. If this happens to you, talk to your doctor right away.

The causes are unclear but may include: sensitivity to hormone changes in the body after childbirth; having previously had depression, especially during pregnancy or after childbirth; difficult or stressful personal relationships; few family members or friends to talk to; other stressful life events during pregnancy or after childbirth.

Any woman can get it, and feeling this way does not mean that you're a bad person. Postpartum depression can be treated with an antidepressant medicine or counseling/therapy.

The **Right** Prescription

Sarah's Story *(Name has been changed to protect patient confidentiality)*
The chief complaint was "depression and anxiety." This was all I knew about the patient before I entered the room. As I opened the door of the exam room, I was met by my patient and her sister. My patient was sitting on the exam table, looking very sad. Her sister was sitting across from her, looking very concerned.

I introduced myself, sat down, and proceeded to hear a story that I have heard repeatedly since being in practice. Different details, but same overall picture.

The patient is a 28-year-old female who got into an argument with her husband the day before her visit. At that time, she experienced an anxiety attack, during which she had difficulty breathing, was shaky, and had difficulty thinking and concentrating. This feeling lasted for a couple of hours before it went away, but she then continued to feel down and depressed. She said that she had been feeling weepy and very emotional over the preceding 5-6 months. She was very irritable and would get upset at things that normally wouldn't bother her. She no longer had interest in doing things she would normally do, like cleaning her house. She normally took pride in her home's appearance, but now, "it wouldn't matter if she didn't clean it, as mold would just have to grow." She had no desire for normal things and felt guilty "about everything." Because her house did not look the way she thought it should, she was feeling very guilty. Not only did the house not look like she wanted, but she didn't look like she wanted, as she experienced poor self-esteem. She was also not sleeping well at night.

The patient has two children (a 5-year-old and a 1-year-old). She started feeling these depressive symptoms when her youngest child was 6-7 months old. She had a history of postpartum depression, first occurring after having her first child. During that time, she had times when she was afraid to even be alone with her son. At that time, she didn't seek help for her condition, stating that she was "good at hiding her feelings." The feeling eventually passed. What kept her this time to not hurt herself was the love that she had for her two children.

Multiple members of her family suffer from anxiety, to include her sister, mother and grandmother. Her sister was a great support to her, as she personally experienced what the patient was now going through and was currently being treated with medication and was in counseling herself.

The patient's other supports are her husband and her faith. She said she attended church and believed in prayer.

While telling me her history, the patient started to cry. Her crying led to her sister's crying as well. My heart went out to her, as it was difficult to see her in so much pain. I was acutely aware of how she felt, because I have felt the same way in my life as well. So, although I knew that she currently felt this way, I knew that I could help her, both with the medicine and counseling that I would prescribe, but also by letting her know that she was not alone. I had been through it, and she had hope.

And hope was what I offered her.

I ordered lab work to rule out any other medical causes that might contribute to her symptoms. After discussing her options, the patient decided to be placed on medication to help her deal with the depression, anxiety, and insomnia that I diagnosed her with. She was also referred for counseling.

Beyond treating her emotional and physical ailment, as a Christian physician, I was able to relate to her on a spiritual level as well. As she told me that she believed in prayer, I asked her if it would be okay if I prayed with her. I know that I am only a physician, but God is the Great Physician, Who she could turn to help her during this time of need. The patient agreed, and she, her sister, and I joined hands to pray. When the prayer was finished, hugs were shared

The **Right** Prescription

and it seemed as though the patient already felt better. Her parting words to me were that I was a "blessing to her on that day." She stated that she now felt relief and that she now had help and hope.

A week later, I called her in follow up. The patient sounded like a new person. Her voice was lighter, as she stated that she was feeling much better, and was tolerating her medications. She had not yet gone to counseling, but was in the process of doing so. All in all, she was in a better place, and is expected to go on and live a happy and fulfilled life, as a wonderful mother to her children.

Case Examples: What have you learned about depression?

Pam's Story

Do you remember the song by Patti LaBelle entitled, "A New Attitude." *I'm feelin' good from my head to my shoes...know where I'm goin' and I know what to do...I tidied up my point of view... I got a new attitude...* I'm in control, *my worries are few....Cause I've got love like I never knew...Ooh, ooh, ooh, ooh, ooh...I got a new attitude.*

I got a new attitude in January, 2011, after battling depression for months prior. Each day, I woke up crying with a deep heaviness on me, not wanting to start my day, fearing what I was going to face, and regretting the things I had to do. Each day, I found myself crying out to the Lord asking for relief from this unhappiness, but to no avail. Each day, I faced people, and pretended that nothing was wrong, while at the same time, holding back tears as to what was really going on. Each day, when I got alone and behind closed doors, the tears flowed, and the feeling of despair, loneliness, and hopelessness weighed heavily on me. I told no one but my husband—even he couldn't help me, though he tried.

How did this all begin?" I can't really tell you, but I strongly believe that fatigue and the "loss of self" had a great deal to do with it. You see, I stay very busy. I am often found trying to juggle twin teens, a husband, and a ministry--never stopping to rest or take time for me.

One day, as I was awakening with the same burden, I heard the Lord say to me, "Go to the doctor". Prior, I had avoided going to the doctor, thinking that I was going to "pray it away", but God told me that I couldn't do this by myself. In obedience, I made an appointment with the doctor, and he told me that what I was suffering from was common for women who carried a great load, like being a mother, a wife, having a job, a ministry, etc. He told me that in order to beat this depression, I had to do something that

The **Right** Prescription

"floats my boat", or in other words, do something for me. We are so busy doing for others that we never stop to do for ourselves. Soon after that, I made a decision that I was coming out of this. I changed my diet and began to exercise. I walked, joined the health club, and took up Zumba, which I love very much. (I eventually lost about 20 pounds.) During this time, I also sought the Lord more, and it was in the midst of my depression, the Lord spoke to my spirit, and "De Novo Woman" was born.

Who is a De Novo Woman? *Luke 13:13 says, "But when Jesus saw her, He called her to Him, and said to her, "Woman, you are loosed from your infirmity," and Mark 5:34 (KJV) reads, "Daughter, thy faith hath made thee whole…"* Therefore, a De Novo Woman is a woman whose desire is to be renewed in all areas of her life, as she is drawn to a closer more intimate relationship with God." I am that De Novo Woman! Might I add that depression still tries to rear his ugly head at me, but I "continue earnestly in prayer" (Colossians 4:2) and I continue to take time for me.

Pam Robinson, Ordained Minister
www.denovoministries.com

Questions:

What were the triggers/contributing factors to Pam's depression?

_____

_____

_____

_____

_____

_____

_____

_____

_____

_____

_____

_____

_____

What depressive symptoms did she experience?

_____

_____

_____

_____

_____

_____

_____

_____

_____

_____

_____

_____

What helped her and brought her back to a place of healing?

_____

_____

_____

_____

_____

_____

_____

_____

_____

_____

_____

_____

The **R**ight Prescription
X

Renee's Story

"I'm just going to take the gift back I bought you for Christmas and you won't get anything." These were my husband's hurtful words. What had he bought me? My emotions were going crazy because my husband wasn't very kind and I worked overtime trying to seek affection and any type outward show of love. "It was a watch but you're not going to get it. Since you said we needed money for other things, I'll just take your watch back!" All I wanted was to see what he'd bought me – I would have been fine with that. As it turned out, I wasn't *fine*, I didn't see the gift and I was about to realize that I'd crossed the thin emotional line that separates sanity from insanity. It was the proverbial "straw" that broke the camel's back and I was a broken woman. How could someone be so mean and insensitive? Why did it matter that much to me?

I was voted the "girl most likely to succeed" by my high school classmates who saw me as successful because of my many achievements in high school and what they assumed I'd accomplish in the future. I had always been a person who liked to succeed at whatever I set my mind to and I rarely failed at any attempt. Success seemed to be my middle name and the more I succeeded at, the more achievements I desired to be added to my list of accomplishments. I had supportive parents who would always attend events I participated in, never discouraged me from dreaming big and they provided the means by which I could continue to grow. I was consumed by academics, extra-curricular activities, a part-time job and regular weekly chores at home. I was a cheerleader, first-chair clarinet in the band, president of my class, member of various clubs, honor society and winner of lots of awards and recognition. I went to church but I didn't serve the Lord or really grow in my faith because I didn't have anyone in my family who patterned the faith walk so I did the best I knew to do – go to church. My overachieving nature was in part (what I later learned) the mask for covering a deeper, more serious emotional challenge – surviving incest. As an incest survivor I was fortunate that my path followed a positive, successful road and that I'd not completely been consumed by self-destructive behavior. What I didn't realize then was that my need to succeed and feel accomplished would be what ultimately left me with "no gas in my emotional tank" and I would come face-to-face with a real emotional breakdown.

Let's revisit the gift issue and my feelings of despair that resulted from the rejection by my husband. I remember how I pleaded in desperation with him to at least tell me something about the gift as if that was what was going to make the pain of rejection disappear. My pleas fell on deaf ears because he was the type individual who thrived on hurting and manipulating anyone who appeared vulnerable. I was extremely vulnerable because for the five years we had known each other, I was always trying to make *right* the many things that were *wrong* about our relationship. I had been subjected to emotional and physical abuse, had to endure countless incidents of humiliation due to his unfaithfulness, and had very low self-esteem. I was a shell of the person I'd been in high school yet I thought I was still the same. My strength was being sucked up by the many futile attempts I'd made to feel loved. I sought validation from him in all areas but what I primarily received was pain and rejection. I spent the majority of the time trying to succeed at having a good relationship because I was groomed to succeed. How could I possibly lose at the first real relationship I'd ever had?

I remember sobbing and walking into our bedroom in our two-bedroom apartment because I'd been crushed emotionally. I'd hit rock bottom and it had taken very little to cause my breakdown. As I walked in the room, I looked up in the closet and saw the holster… the gun…the answer. I didn't think about shooting him or hurting myself, but the very presence of the gun sent a chill down my spine. I feared what that gun could represent. I immediately picked up the phone and called a mental health hotline because that's all I knew to do. I could not stop crying. The counselor who took my call asked me a few questions and wanted to know if I could drive to the crisis center. Through my sobs I said 'yes' and I let her know I would be on my way. The drive was a complete fog; not the wisest thing I should have done in my state of mind. But, I made it safely there and was interviewed by the intake counselor and admitted within 15 minutes after my arrival.

I was already the mother of a toddler and I don't remember where my child was when I left home to drive to the mental health facility.

- I was a *mess*.
- I was a *Christian*.
- I was *depressed*.
- I was *hurting*.

I was in a mental hospital for the first time in my life. I hadn't succeeded at balancing emotions to prevent my breakdown because I didn't understand what had been brewing for so long inside me. Outer appearances were in place; inner feelings were in shambles. My first night in the facility was uneventful and I slept well even though I shared the room with a complete stranger. I was awakened in the morning to the sound of water and realized that my roommate had decided to urinate on the floor in our room instead of going to the bathroom. With my eyes opened long enough to realize where the sound was coming from, I realized that I wasn't the least bit bothered by her actions and I don't think she was the least bit phased by my existence either. I dozed back off.

Later in the afternoon after meeting with my counselor, I joined all the other patients in the day room for rest and recreation. Some people appeared to have more extreme outward manifestations of their inward struggles, but nothing really bothered me. I began drawing a picture and while doing so I felt an incredible feeling of pressure come over me. It was like someone had a hand on each one of my shoulders and was pressing inward. I looked up and my husband was standing in the doorway of the day room! He'd reluctantly come to meet with me and the counselor to discuss my condition. In our meeting, he was resistant, arrogant, uncaring and made it clear that he would not agree to work things out while I remained in the facility. We said our 'good-byes' and he left. No hugs and kisses, no warmth…just good-bye.

Later that afternoon I met with my counselor again. This time it was for the purpose of letting him know that I wanted to leave the facility. That request was initially met with opposition because he didn't feel like I was ready to leave due to the condition I was in when I arrived the night before. I explained the feeling that had come over me earlier that day when I was in the day room and that I realized where my problems stemmed from – my spouse. I told him that if I didn't leave that day I probably would never leave. I was free. I was safe. I was numb. Who couldn't get used to that? I knew that for the sake of my son, I couldn't get used to that. I'd also discovered – through blood work that was done during my intake – that I would be giving birth to a precious child in about seven months. So with that statement, he signed the papers for my release. I called my husband and left the facility to face the real-life challenges that awaited me at home.

As I have grown in the Lord I have come to recognize all the warning signs that were so prevalent in my battle with depression and ultimate nervous breakdown. I describe my breakdown like running out of gas in your vehicle. If you've ever run out of gas you know how far down the needle goes before your tank is empty. It could be well past the 'E' and you have that extra little cushion time before your car eventually stops. That's how I was. I was way past 'E' in my emotional tank because I'd not realized I was so low. Now I do. I can tell when I'm heading for 'E' and I can use the tools I didn't know to use back then to fill me up and jumpstart my emotions for the long haul.

The  Prescription

Questions:

What were the triggers/contributing factors to Renee's depression?

_____
_____
_____
_____
_____
_____
_____
_____
_____
_____
_____
_____
_____

What depressive symptoms did Renee experience?

_____
_____
_____
_____
_____
_____
_____
_____
_____
_____
_____
_____
_____

What helped her and brought her back to a place of healing?

_____

_____

_____

_____

_____

_____

_____

_____

_____

_____

_____

_____

_____

_____

It's Ok to Cry!

John 11:35: "Jesus wept."
Psalm 30:5: "Weeping may endure for a night, but joy will come in the morning!"

One of the lessons that I have learned from the recent passing of my mother is that it is ok to cry. I say this because I think, a lot of times, we erroneously believe that crying, or showing any kind of emotion, is a sign of weakness, especially for a Christian. Some might see it as a sign of loss of faith or hopelessness.

This is not true, however, because we are called to be Christ-like— as He was, so shall we be. In the story of Lazarus' resurrection from the dead, Jesus was not unfeeling and without emotion. No, when he was brought to where Lazarus' body was laid, Jesus wept. His weeping was not a sign of weakness, but showed the Jews who were around Him "how much He loved [Lazarus]." (John 11:36)

I am so glad that we serve a God Who is not distant or estranged

The **Right** Prescription

from us. He not only cares for us, but He feels as we feel, even our pain and sorrow. Not only is it ok to cry, the Bible says that God is close to the brokenhearted, and that He bottles up and collects every tear that we shed.

I will not leave you in tears, however, because today's second verse says we have a hope that our weeping may endure for a night, but joy will come in the morning. One day, God will wipe every tear from our eyes. There will be no more death or mourning or crying or pain (Revelations 21:4) because God will make everything new! (Revelations 21:5)

Even before Christ returns, we still have a hope because those who sow in tears will reap with songs of joy (Psalm 126:5). I like what the Life Application Bible says…"Grief is not a permanent condition. Our tears can be seeds that will grow into a harvest of joy because God is able to bring good out of tragedy." When burdened by sorrow, we must remember that our times of grief will end, and that we will again find joy. We must be patient as we wait. God's great harvest of joy is coming!

So, don't be afraid or ashamed of your tears. Jesus knows, cares, and cries with you. But, although you may currently feel despair, don't stay there—your harvest of joy is coming!

The Final Prognosis

It is my hope that in reading this book you realize that there is help for those suffering from depression. Both medically and spiritually, there is hope. If you "found yourself" in what you have read, take heart. There is a reason you are reading this book. God is ready to help and heal you. All you need to do is do your part, and ask. The Word says that we have not because we ask not (James 4:2). Ask God to show you what you need to do and who you need to go to for help. Have faith that He will, and then DO IT. Remember, faith without works is dead (James 2:17). Don't just acknowledge your depression, DO SOMETHING so that you can be healed.

I always tell my patients that the best thing I can do for them is pray. Prayer is the best medicine that I can give. The first step of hope in your treatment, is obtaining the hope of salvation. I pray that if you do not know the Lord as your Savior that you come to know Him now.

It's as easy as A...B...C

Acknowledge that you are a sinner, meaning that you have done wrong in your life that has separated you from God;

Believe that Jesus died on the cross in your place for your sins, so that you could be brought back into right relationship with God

Confess those sins by simply saying that you did them, you are sorry for them, and you want Jesus to forgive you for them. That's it—you are now saved!

I also pray that the Lord bless you in this journey of healing. May He give you peace, comfort, and strength in your valley. May He bless you with good healthcare providers, clergy, family and friends to support you during this time. May you arise out of this dark pit to the wealthy and blessed place that God will bring you to. Truly, your weeping may endure for a night, but your joy will come in the morning!

That is my prayer for you. God bless you always!

Janine Scott, MD

Read one pill a day and you may keep the doctor — and your blues — away!

- Hebrews 13:5: "For [God] Himself said, "I will never leave you, nor will I ever forsake you."

- Romans 8:1: "There is therefore now no condemnation to those who are in Christ Jesus."

- Philippians 1:6: "And I am sure that God, Who began the good work within you, will keep right on helping you grow in His grace until His task within you is finally finished on that day when Jesus Christ returns."

- Lamentations 3:12-13: "Yet there is one ray of hope; [God's] compassion never ends. It is only the Lord's mercies that have kept us from complete destruction. Great is His faithfulness; His loving kindness begins afresh each day."

- Exodus 15:26 "…for I am the Lord, Who heals you."

- Romans 8:28: "And we know that all things work together for the good of those who love God and are called according to His purpose."

- Psalm 46:1-2: "God is our refuge and strength, a very present help in times of trouble. Therefore I will not fear, though the earth be moved and though the mountains fall into the midst of the sea."

- Jeremiah 29:11: "For I know the plans I have for you, says the Lord; plans for good and not for evil, to give you a future and a hope."

- Jeremiah 31:13: "I will turn their mourning into joy and I will comfort them and make them rejoice, for their captivity with all its sorrows will be behind them."

- Psalm 34:15: "For the eyes of the Lord are intently watching all who live good lives, and He gives attention when they cry to Him."

- Psalm 34:18-19: "The Lord is close to those whose hearts are breaking...the good man does not escape all troubles-he has them too. But, the Lord helps him in each and every one."

- Psalm 42:4-5: "Take courage, my soul! Why be downcast? Why be discouraged and sad? Hope in God! I shall yet praise Him again. Yes. I shall again praise Him for His help. O my soul, don't be discouraged. Don't be upset. Expect God to act! For I know that I shall again have plenty of reason to praise Him for all that He will do. He is my help! He is my God."

- Psalm 139:17: "How precious are thy thoughts unto me, O God! How great is the sum of them."

- Psalm 23:4: "Yea, though I walk through the valley of the shadow of death, I will fear no evil: for thou art with me; thy rod and thy staff they comfort me."

- 3 John 2: "Beloved, I wish above all things that thou mayest prosper and be in health, even as thy soul prospereth."

- Philippians 4:8: "Whatsoever things are true, whatsoever things are honest, whatsoever things are just, whatsoever things are pure, whatsoever things are lovely, whatsoever things are of good report; if there by any virtue, and if there be any praise, think on these things."

- Romans 12:2: "And be not conformed to this world; but be ye transformed by the renewing of your mind."

- Psalm 126:5: "They that sow in tears shall reap in joy."

- Hebrews 4:15: "For we have not an high priest which cannot be touched with the feeling of our infirmities;

but was in all points tempted like we are, yet without sin."

- Nehemiah 8:10: "Don't be sorry; for the joy of the Lord is your strength."

- 2 Corinthians 1:3-4: "Blessed be God, even the Father of our Lord Jesus Christ, the Father of mercies, and the God of all comfort; Who comforteth us in all our tribulation, that we may comfort others with the same comfort that we have received from God."

- 1 Corinthians 2:9: "Eye hath not seen, nor ear heard, neither has entered into the heart of man, the things which God has in store for those that love Him."

- 2 Timothy 1:7: "For God hath not given us the spirit of fear; but of power, and of love, and of a sound mind."

- 1 Corinthians 2:16: "But we have the mind of Christ."

- Psalm 30:5: "Weeping may endure for a night, but joy cometh in the morning."

- Isaiah 61:2-3: "...to comfort all that mourn...to give them beauty for ashes, the oil of joy for mourning, the garment of praise for the spirit of heaviness."

- 1 John 4:16: "God is love."

- Ecclesiastes 3:1, 4: "To everything there is a season, and a time to every purpose under the heaven; a time to weep, and a time to laugh; a time to mourn, and a time to dance."

- Luke 6:21: "Blessed are ye that weep now; for ye shall laugh."

- John 11:35: "Jesus wept."

- Isaiah 35:10: "They shall obtain joy and gladness, and sorry and mourning shall flee away."

Depression Resources

National Suicide Prevention Lifeline:

24- hour, toll-free, confidential crises hotline for anyone (you or a loved one) who may be suicidal or in psychological crisis.
(800)273-TALK (8255); Hotline for Spanish Speakers: (888)628-9454; TTY Hotline: (800)799-4TTY (4889)
National Institute of Mental Health (NIMH): Federal agency that provides mental health information, supports and conducts research on mental and behavioral disorders.
Public Information and Communications Branch
6001 Executive Boulevard, Room 8184, MSC 9663
Bethesda, MD 20892-9663
1-866-615-6464
TTY: 1-866-415-8051
nimhinfo@nih.gov

National Alliance on Mental Illness (NAMI):

Largest national grassroots organization dedicated to improving the lives of people with mental illness and their families. Provides support, education, advocacy, and research for people living with mental illness. Local chapters in every state.
2107 Wilson Blvd., Suite 300
Arlington, VA 22201-3042
1-703-524-7600
TDD: 1-703-516-7227
Help Line: 1-800-950-NAMI (6264)
info@nami.org

Depression and Bipolar Support Alliance (DBSA):

Nation's leading non-profit organization supporting individuals with depression and bipolar disorder. Has over 1,000 support groups nationwide, educational materials and programs.
730 N. Franklin Street, Suite 501
Chicago, Illinois 60610-7224
1-800-826-3632
info@bsalliance.org

American Academy of Family Physician's Patient Education Resource:
http://www.aafp.org/afp/2002/0915/p1051.html
http://www.aafp.org/afp/2006/1015/p1395.html

Postpartum Depression

American Academy of Family Physician's Patient Education Resource:
http://familydoctor.org/379.xml,   http://familydoctor.org/871.xml,
http://www.aafp.org/afp/2010/1015/p939.html
American College of Obstetricians and Gynecologists:
http://www.acog.org/publications/patient_education/bp091.cfm

U.S. Department of Health and Human Services: Office on Women's Health:
http://ww.womenshealth.gov/faq/depression-pregnancy.cfm

Postpartum Support International:
http://www.postpartum.net